Hairy Maclary's Hat Tricks

Lynley Dodd

PUFFIN

SWOOOSH
went the wind
in the tops of the trees,
swishing the branches
and tossing the leaves.
It whipped around corners
and blew over bins,
it buffeted birds
into spirals and spins.
A blusterous, gusterous,
dusterous day,
but Hairy Maclary
was ready
to play.

He scooped up his skimmer
and carried it down
to the edge of the park
at the far end of town.
The wind was so restless,
its buffets so strong,
that it flapped him
and slapped him
and zapped him
along.

He waited for someone
to stop
and to play ...

but everyone said,
'We're TOO BUSY
today!'

Along came Miss Plum.
She patted his nose.
'Maybe,' she said,
'just a couple of throws.'

WHIZZ
went the skimmer
and off like a shot,
went Hairy Maclary,
post-haste,
from the spot.
He hurtled so fast
over pathway and creek,
that his legs were a blur
and his tail was
a streak.

THEN
with a swoop
and a flurry of black,
he caught it
and carried it
ALL the way
back.

ZING
went the skimmer,
high over a seat,
but Hairy Maclary
had wings on his feet.
He zoomed like a rocket,
he galloped and sped,
over railings and grass
and begonia bed.

THEN
with a swoop
and a flurry of black,
he caught it
and carried it
ALL the way
back.

Up at the top
in the summery sun,
the wind was enjoying
some frolicsome fun.
It played with the hats,
all the dresses
and veils,
it hassled the hairdos
and tangled
the tails.

Grandmother Pugh
was a vision in blue,
from the top of her head
to the bow on her shoe.
Her hat was a riot
of ribbon and lace,
roses and feathers
that tickled her face.
She clung to it bravely
but – doom and dismay –
the wind whistled through it
and blew it
away.

Hairy Maclary,
as quick as a flash,
was off on a desperate,
daredevil
dash.
Like lightning he scooted,
skedaddle-skeddoo,
while faster and faster,
the hat simply
FLEW.

He chased it through marigolds,
over a frond,
straight through the hedge
to the edge
of the pond.

THEN
with a swoop
and a flurry of black,
he caught it
and carried it …

ALL the way
back.

PUFFIN BOOKS

Published by the Penguin Group: London, New York,
Australia, Canada, India, Ireland, New Zealand and South Africa
Penguin Books Limited, Registered Offices: 80 Strand, London WC2R 0RL, England

puffinbooks.com

Published in New Zealand by Mallinson Rendel Publishers Limited 2007
Published in Great Britain in Puffin Books 2007
1 3 5 7 9 10 8 6 4 2
Copyright © Lynley Dodd, 2007
All rights reserved
The moral right of the author/illustrator has been asserted
Made and printed in China
ISBN: 978–0–141–38376–7